Dangerous Cargo

The driver heard a crash.

He shined his flashlight on the rear of the truck and saw that the panel of the cargo compartment was open.

"I was sure I fastened that —" His breath caught in his throat.

In the flashlight beam was a pair of eyes.

Yellow eyes.

Inhuman eyes.

The driver dropped the flashlight.

He aimed his gun and fired. Again and again and again.

THE ⊗ FILES™

E.B.E.

a novel by Les Martin

based on the television series
The X-Files created by Chris Carter
based on the teleplay
written by Glen Morgan and James Wong

HarperTrophy
A Division of HarperCollinsPublishers

To Tamar,
the gray ghost

E.B.E.

Chapter ONE

Stars filled the night sky over Iraq. They were dazzling as diamonds above the dark desert. There were no clouds or moon or haze of pollution to blur their brilliance. The drifting smoke from oil fires in nearby Kuwait was history. The Gulf War that had set the region ablaze had ended years ago. Only one thing disturbed the peaceful scene—the vapor trail of a jet plane streaking across the sky.

The plane was a Tupelov TV-22 "Blinder" attack jet—one of Russia's most advanced fighters, given to Iraq before the Gulf War. It had been one of the few to survive the crushing defeat at the hands of America and her allies.

Its pilot could thank his lucky stars that he had survived as well. Sadoun Janadi had still been in training when the war ended. By the time he had won his wings, the sky was safe again. He could fly patrols with little worry of attack. He could relax behind his air mask and enjoy the beauty of the night.

At heart, Janadi was a poet. He gazed at the stars, some shining alone, others in thick clusters.

He tried to think of words to capture their splendor, as Arab poets had for thousands of years.

Suddenly Janadi stopped being a poet.

He was all fighter pilot, with a job to do.

His job was to protect Iraq from air intruders. He spotted one now.

It was still far away, as small as the stars around it. But it was swiftly getting bigger and brighter. Seconds later he could make out its shape, like a cigar. Its lights were strobing different colors, red, green, and blue.

Janadi looked at his radar screen to confirm his sighting.

The screen showed nothing.

Janadi shot a look at the object again.

It was moving across the sky in a razor-sharp straight line. As Janadi watched, it stopped and hung motionless. But its lights continued their strobing.

Janadi's brow furrowed. His radar must be on the blink. He wasn't surprised. The air force was short of parts, not to mention mechanics. He'd have to depend on his eyes.

He squinted at the object. He was trained to identify every known kind of aircraft, both hostile and friendly. But this one was new to him.

He snapped on his radio and contacted his home base.

"Al-Hadithi here," a voice answered in Arabic.

Good, Janadi thought. He knew Al-Hadithi. A very reliable radar technician. Not like some of the new ones, pressed into service to replace those killed in the war.

"Base, this is Patrol Six," Janadi said. "Request ID on object twenty-five miles from my position bearing three-forty."

There was a pause.

Then, over crackling static, Al-Hadithi responded, "Negative on object. No sign of anything in that area. Are you sure your bearings are correct?"

Janadi rechecked his instruments.

"Absolutely correct," he said. "That is, if my instruments are working. Please take another radar reading."

Again there was a pause. Again Al-Hadithi reported, "Negative. No object sighted."

Janadi bit his lip. He never did trust Russian radar. He looked out his window again.

The object was gone.

"Hello, hello," Al-Hadithi said. "Do you still have visual contact with unknown object?"

"No. I have lost it," Janadi said. "But I am positive it was there a moment ago. I—"

That was as far as he got.

Blinding light exploded almost on top of his plane. A deafening *whoosh* drowned out the radio.

Janadi's heart seemed to stop. He sat frozen at his controls.

Suddenly the light and sound vanished.

Janadi realized he had been holding his breath. He was letting out a sigh of relief when he heard Al-Hadithi screaming over the radio, "Radar shows you are under attack! Objects swarming around you at high speed. Incredibly high speed. Take evasive action and go into attack mode."

Janadi needed no prompting. He was already zooming upward and zigzagging. His eyes narrowed as he peeled off into an attack on whatever was flying below.

He couldn't see it. But he had an electronic weapons guidance system to do his seeing for him. Its light began flashing.

"I'm locked in on target!" he announced over the radio.

"You are cleared to commence firing," Al-Hadithi told him.

Janadi pressed his right wing weapon release button. He watched a heat-seeking missile shoot from his plane.

Seconds later the sky was lit by a tremendous yellow-and-orange fireball.

"It's a hit!" Janadi exulted as he banked his craft up and away from the flames. "I got him."

"Good work," Al-Hadithi told him. "Please return to base and give full report."

Only then did Janadi realize that the night's work was far from over. He had no idea whom or what he had hit. He wouldn't have a clue until someone found the pieces below. He could only pray it turned out to be an enemy.

Janadi sighed. He braced himself for a long session of questions without answers back at the base. He could think of only one thing he had going for him. He couldn't be blamed for a mistaken kill when nobody knew the victim.

"Wha—" mumbled Sergeant Eustace Miller. A loud bang woke him from a pleasant dream of home.

"Some kind of sonic boom," Specialist First Class Horace Keller said from a nearby cot. His voice was groggy with sleep.

"Never heard no boom like that before," Miller said. "We better take a look."

"And you was just complaining today how dull it was around here," Keller said as he pulled on a pair of fatigue pants.

Neither of the two American soldiers wasted time putting on their boots before they headed out of their hut. They belonged to NATO forces in Turkey keeping watch on the Iraqi border, in case the Iraqis hadn't learned their lesson. This was the first sign of trouble since they had arrived four months earlier.

They stopped as soon as they were out the door. In the woods a few hundred feet away was the wreck of something burning.

"Looks like a crashed jet," Miller said.

"I'll get the fire extinguisher," said Keller.

"You know our orders. First we have to report it, without delay," said Miller. "Anyway, not much chance anything's still alive in it."

"Yeah," said Keller. "Besides, dollars to doughnuts the pilot ejected."

They went back into the hut. Their hut was primitive, but their radio was state-of-the-art. A touch of a button, and Miller was in contact with headquarters.

"Southern Crescent to Red Crescent," he said. "We got a downed aircraft at the edge of camp. Maybe one of ours."

The voice on the radio replied, "Southern Crescent, that's a negative. We have nothing in the sky at this time."

"Well, we got something burning here on the ground," Miller said. "Advise Medivac unit to be on the alert. They may have to handle injured personnel. We're checking out the wreck and the surrounding area now."

"Report immediately on your findings," the voice commanded.

"Yes, sir," Miller said, and turned off the set.

"I've got the extinguisher," said Keller.

"I'll take the first aid kit—in case we find anyone alive anywhere," said Miller.

Outside the hut, Miller stared up at the sky.

"What the devil is that?" he asked.

Above them a bright, strobing light flashed red, green, and blue.

"Maybe a shooting star," Keller guessed.

"Shooting stars don't just hang there like that," Miller said.

"Who knows?" said Keller with a shrug. "All kinds of weird things in this part of the world."

"Yeah," Miller agreed. "Anyway, we can't stand around digging the light show. We got orders to check out the wreck."

"Well, remember what they told us in special training," said Keller. "Expect the unexpected—and be ready for it."

"Right," said Miller, as they warily approached the wreck in the woods. "Except how can you be ready for something you can't even guess?"

Meanwhile, above them the light still hung, strobing a coded message no human could decipher.

Chapter **TWO**

A few nights later and half a world away, the stars shined bright over Tennessee. But the driver of the eighteen-wheeler roaring down Route 100 wasn't looking at them. His eyes were glued to the road stretching empty as far as he could see. Now and then he rubbed his eyes to keep them open and ran his hand along the two-day stubble on his cheek to keep himself alert.

He had been driving a long, long time, and the pills he had popped to keep awake were wearing off. He would have liked to stop for some shut-eye by the side of the road. But orders were orders, and his were to deliver his cargo without delay. He had his job because he knew how to take orders, whatever they were. And it might cost him more than his job if he didn't carry them out.

He read a road sign as he roared by it. REAGAN, TENNESSEE. 40 MILES.

Over a half-hour drive, he thought, even ignoring the speed limit. He turned up the volume on his AM radio to keep himself from nodding off. The blast of sound drowned out the boring conversations crackling over his CB receiver.

8

Loud applause thundered through the driver's cabin. A hearty voice announced, "From Opryland, it's the Grand Ole Opry on WSM radio 650. Brought to you by Goody's Headache Powder . . ."

"Come on, cut the talking," the driver said, his finger tapping impatiently on the wheel. "Start the music—I need a real good foot-stomper."

But suddenly the program faded into static.

"What the—?" The driver fiddled with the dial. Anger flushed his cheeks. He didn't like things going wrong. Not on this job.

At the same time he glanced at the seat beside him, his eyes like a nervous cat's. That space was called the shotgun seat. Right now it lived up to its name. A Mossberg 500 12-gauge pump shotgun with an assault grip rode beside him, in quick and easy reach.

The static would not go away. It rubbed against his brain like sandpaper. Grimacing, he gave up playing with the dial. He jabbed the radio off.

In its place, he heard the babble of voices coming over the CB.

Usually this time of night those voices were relaxed, rambling, as if they were talking to each other in a dream.

Tonight they had the pitch of panic, as if that dream were a nightmare.

The first one he heard gasped, "It was . . . it

was . . . cigar-shaped . . . red and green lights . . . and traveling fast as the devil . . ."

A second voice cut in, "I seen three of them flying over Chester County! Sure as I'm sitting here shaking in my boots!"

A third caller announced, "Right! Right! Six troopers were chasing them down Twenty-two!"

Then the voices were drowned out by a siren howling outside. The driver's head swiveled toward the ear-splitting noise. A state police car shot by the truck as if the eighteen-wheeler were standing still.

The siren faded as the cop car sped out of sight down the road. The first voice came over the CB again. It was screaming, "I see one now! It's over the water tower!"

"What the blue blazes is going down?" the driver wondered, waiting for the next report.

Then the CB went dead.

So did the truck lights. And the engine. The giant vehicle rolled gently to a stop.

Frantically, the driver tried the ignition. It was dead. He flicked his CB off and on again. No luck there, either.

His eyes narrowed. He made up his mind. With one hand he took a flashlight out of a front compartment. With the other he picked up the shotgun.

Cautiously he climbed down from the driver's

cabin. He stood under the stars on the dark and empty highway, looking in every direction.

He stiffened. A humming came from above.

It was loud. But not loud enough to keep the driver from hearing his own panting breath and the pounding of his heart.

Shotgun at the ready, he whirled around, hunting a target, to the left, to the right, in front, behind, down, and up.

Then he saw it—whatever it was. A shape blotting out a multitude of stars. But all he could tell for sure was that it was big, very big, and black as the night.

The driver pumped his weapon with the hand that held the flashlight.

Then he heard a crash.

He shined his flashlight on the rear of the truck and saw that the panel of the cargo compartment was open.

"I was sure I fastened that—" His breath caught in his throat.

In the flashlight beam was a pair of eyes.

Yellow eyes.

Inhuman eyes.

The driver dropped the flashlight.

He aimed his gun and fired. Again and again and again.

Chapter THREE

Special Agent Fox Mulder stooped down. He picked up a shotgun shell casing from the road.

Straightening, he glanced at it. Then he silently passed it to his partner, Special Agent Dana Scully.

It was a chilly day in Tennessee. A late-autumn wind chased billowing clouds across a deep blue sky. The sun played peekaboo, flooding Route 100 with bright light one moment, sweeping it into shadow the next. The leaves rustled in the trees lining the highway where the two FBI agents stood.

Mulder and Scully had flown in from Washington, D.C., before dawn. A phone call from FBI Head-quarters had roused Mulder from sleep in the middle of the night. He'd instantly called Scully. Sometimes it took time to decide if a case belonged in the X-files. But this case left no doubts. Too many weird things had happened that night in Tennessee.

Scully made sure she was the one to get behind the steering wheel of the rental car they picked up in Memphis. One of them had to keep cool, and, as usual, she was the one.

Now she cast a cold eye on the cartridge Mulder handed her.

"From the way the trucker described it, the so-called eyes he shot at could have been a mountain lion's," she told Mulder. "They still roam the hill country around here."

"Anything's possible," Mulder agreed in a flat voice.

"Mountain lions have been known to . . ." Scully began. But Mulder was already walking away from her, back to their rental car.

As Scully watched, he took two stopwatches from his briefcase. He carefully set both of them to the same time. Then he laid one on the car seat and slipped the other into his pocket. He picked up his briefcase and headed back to the red chalk marks on the highway that showed where the truck had stalled the night before.

Scully knew better than to ask any questions. She knew she'd find out what Mulder was up to soon enough. When Mulder sensed something strange, he moved fast.

For the moment, all she could do was comment, "The National Weather Service reported fast-moving electrical storms in the area. They could have caused lightning in certain isolated spots."

"Possibly," said Mulder. He had taken a camera out of his briefcase and was snapping photos of the area.

"It is feasible that the truck was struck by

lightning," Scully persisted. "It could have caused an electrical failure."

"Feasible," Mulder echoed as he knelt on the road. With a thin metal scraper he collected a sample of gray dust coating the asphalt. He deposited the sample in a small container the size of a film canister. He put the canister into a labeled plastic bag.

"There is a logical explanation for everything that happened," Scully continued. "I suggest we begin with that premise. Then, if that leads to a dead end, we can move on to a less likely path of investigation."

Mulder didn't bother answering. He was taking a small general-survey radiation detector out of his briefcase.

As he began to sweep the area, Scully said, "There's a marsh over there. The lights the driver saw may have been swamp gas."

"Swamp gas?" Mulder responded vaguely. The needle on his detector registered 0.1 mR/h.

Scully looked over his shoulder at the radiation reading.

"Barely above normal," she noted. "Swamp gas is a natural phenomenon, quite common in swampy areas," she went on. "Decaying plant life and other organic matter create the chemicals phosphine and methane. They rise into the air and combine. The result ignites globes of blue flame."

"That happens to me when I eat chili cheese

dogs," said Mulder as he moved down the road, sweeping with his detector.

He stopped. He looked at the detector, then at Scully.

Radiation read 0.5 mR/h.

Mulder waited a moment for Scully to come up with an explanation for the sharp rise.

She couldn't.

"How can a dozen witnesses, including a squad of police vehicles in three counties, get hysterical over swamp gas?" Mulder demanded.

"It's hard to . . . that is to say, it may be difficult . . . at least at first glance . . ." Scully fumbled for a response, then gave up and shrugged.

"I've investigated multiple sightings of unidentified flying objects all over the country," Mulder said. "Chesapeake Bay. The Okoboji Lakes. Area Fifty-one in Nevada. But you know about them as well as I. You've had a chance to check them out in the X-files."

"I've read the reports," Scully agreed.

"None of them has as much supportive evidence as this one," said Mulder, his voice rising. "Eyewitness testimony. Exhaust residue from unknown craft. Radiation levels five times the norm."

"None of that evidence is absolutely conclusive," Scully declared, trying to sound firm.

Mulder merely sighed and carefully put his equipment and evidence back into his briefcase.

When he was finished, he returned with Scully to the car.

"For me, the only question is, why was this one truck driver singled out for contact—or for attack?" he persisted.

Scully put the key into the ignition. Before turning it, she said, "Mulder, let's talk common sense. Isn't it more likely that a dead-tired truck driver got swept up by all the wild talk on his CB? Especially if he was taking pills to keep awake? Couldn't he have blasted away at hallucinations?"

Mulder didn't answer.

Her hand still on the ignition key, Scully pressed her point home. "After all, the road *can* play tricks on you."

Mulder still didn't answer.

Instead, with his left hand he fished out the stopwatch he had put in his pocket. With his right hand he picked up the stopwatch he had kept in the car.

"The road can play tricks," Mulder said. "But not like this."

Scully turned to look at the watches.

The watch in his left hand was two minutes faster than the one in his right.

She looked out the window at the empty highway, trying to see where two minutes had gone.

She saw only sunlight and shadows, and heard the howling of a rising wind.

She shivered.

"Let's go see the truck driver," Mulder said. "Time's a-wasting."

Chapter FOUR

"Name?" Mulder asked.

"Ranheim. Greg Ranheim," the truck driver answered. "Look, I told this all to the cops already. I gave them the whole story. You just gotta check with them."

Mulder, with Scully standing behind him, was sitting across from Ranheim at a battered oak table in the bare-bones interrogation room of the local police station. A hooded light hanging from the ceiling glared down on the table, leaving the rest of the room in darkness. The tabletop was bare except for an orange plastic water pitcher and two orange plastic glasses.

Scully was taking notes in shorthand. She had already written: *Subject of interrogation is about thirty-five, six feet tall, and medium build. He has a badly trimmed mustache and several days' growth of beard. He has a skin rash of undetermined origin on his forehead, upper left cheek, and back of both hands. He displays flulike symptoms of coughing and heavy perspiration.*

Now she added: *Subject shows definite signs of hostility and lack of cooperation.*

"We are not part of the local police force," Mulder told Ranheim. "We are federal investigators, making an independent inquiry. We want to double-check all details."

Ranheim gave a rasping cough into his hand and then wiped the sweat from his forehead.

"You're not gonna find out anything because there's nothing to find out," he said. "What you should do is tell these cops to let me out of here. They got no cause to hold me."

"The official charge is 'firing a weapon on a county road,'" Mulder said.

"Yeah, that's what they told me," Ranheim growled. "But it's all horse manure. I'm an army vet. I know how to handle a gun."

A cough racked Ranheim again. His whole upper body shook. He gripped the table edge to steady himself.

Mulder poured water into a glass and pushed it toward Ranheim. The truck driver started to pick it up. Then he gave it a suspicious look and pushed it away, shaking his head.

Scully noted: *Subject seems unduly apprehensive. Possibility of paranoid tendencies.*

"Look, get me out of here," Ranheim said. "I didn't do nothing. And I got a job to do."

"First things first, Mr. Ranheim," Mulder said.

19

"I'd appreciate your help. Please tell me more about what happened last night. I found the police report rather sketchy about your . . ." Mulder paused, then finished, "your encounter."

Ranheim scratched the rash on his forehead. He kept scratching until the skin turned red, almost to the point of bleeding.

"I already been through this," he complained again.

"Once more, please," Mulder said.

"Then will you spring me?"

"Please answer my questions," Mulder repeated.

Ranheim sighed and rubbed his neck in discomfort.

"The object—what did it look like?" Mulder prompted.

"It was round," Ranheim finally said. "Like a saucer. And it had lights, green and orange, flashing like a Christmas tree."

Mulder glanced at the police report on his lap.

"Last night you stated it was cigar-shaped and black," Mulder said.

"Round, square, cigar-shaped. Black, red, green. What's the big deal?" Ranheim griped. "Look, I didn't ask for this to happen. I was minding my own business. Speaking of which, I got a shipment of auto parts to deliver or else my boss will—"

Another spell of coughing cut off his words.

Scully waited until it subsided. Then she asked, "Mr. Ranheim, pardon me for asking, but how long have you had that cough?"

Ranheim looked at her through narrowed eyes. "Why do you want to know?" he demanded.

"Just concerned," Scully said. Then she said, "You mentioned you were a veteran."

"What's that got to do with anything?" Ranheim wanted to know.

"The cough, signs of fever, skin rash—they're all symptoms of the so-called Gulf War Syndrome," said Scully, who had earned a medical degree before going into the FBI.

Ranheim stiffened. "I was never in the Gulf War," he said sharply, almost angrily.

Mulder leaned forward, locking gazes with Ranheim. "So tell me, how long have you—not been yourself?"

"Since last night," Ranheim said, spitting out the words. "You get thrown in the jug for no good reason—and you see how good you feel."

Mulder decided to press harder. He was about to ask his next question when a man in a charcoal-gray suit, white shirt, and striped tie entered the room. His black shoes gleamed in the overhead light as he marched to the table.

"Mr. Ranheim, I'm Police Chief Rivers," the man said, ignoring Mulder and Scully. "Please forgive the misunderstanding. We can find no charges against you. Your truck's been squared away. You may go."

"About time," said Ranheim, getting up from the table as Mulder and Scully watched with open mouths.

Mulder recovered first. "I'd like to examine the truck before he goes," he said to the police chief.

"That will not be necessary," Rivers informed him.

"This man has had a possible close encounter with an unidentified flying object." Mulder tried to keep his voice calm. "His vehicle very well may have important trace evidence, and I merely want to—"

Ranheim grabbed his coat and headed for the door.

Mulder called to him. "Sir, may I ask you a few more—"

Ranheim left. Mulder started to go after him— only to find Rivers standing in his way. The police chief was a big man, built like a football lineman.

"This man is no longer in custody and should not be harassed further," Rivers said in a rock-hard voice.

"But—"

The police chief cut Mulder off. "You have gotten all that you are going to get out of our office. We will no longer cooperate with your investigation."

Mulder did not trust himself to speak. What he felt like saying would only burn all bridges between him and the local law.

Scully spoke for him. "Chief Rivers, just tell me—why?"

Rivers refused to meet her eyes.

He cleared his throat, shrugged, and muttered, "Just . . . go away."

Then he was out the door, leaving Mulder and Scully alone with their questions.

Scully said, "What is happening here? What do you think is behind—"

She got no further.

Mulder put his finger to his lips.

His meaning was clear.

Scully glanced around the bare room.

It was just an ordinary interrogation room in a typical small-town cop station. There had to be thousands like it all over the country. It was as American as apple pie.

Did Mulder really think this room was bugged?

The idea was crazy, but—

But Scully had to admit, sometimes Mulder was right.

Chapter FIVE

Two hours later Scully and Mulder were waiting at the car rental counter in the Memphis airport. They were returning their car before boarding a flight back to Washington.

Mulder was still brooding over having let Ranheim get away. "I should have been quicker and stopped him. I should have seen that somebody had gotten to Rivers. I'm as sure of that as I am that Ranheim was hiding something. You could see him sweat."

Scully tried to calm him. "I agree Ranheim was acting strange. But he was sick."

"He said he became sick last night," Mulder said, as Scully checked the car rental bill.

"I doubt his symptoms could have appeared so quickly," said Scully, taking a pen from her purse and signing the form.

"You still think he was suffering from Gulf War Syndrome?" asked Mulder.

"I can't be positive, but there were striking similarities."

"I hope you realize, Agent Scully, that our government claims the Gulf War Syndrome does not

24

exist," Mulder said wryly. "Are you actually doubt-ing your own leaders?"

Scully was about to reply when someone tapped her on the shoulder.

She turned and saw a harried-looking woman with two small children.

"Pardon me," the woman said. "Can I borrow your pen for a minute? I can't seem to find mine, and the one on the counter doesn't work."

"Sure, no problem," said Scully, handing her the pen. The woman flashed her a grateful smile before trying to fill out a rental form while keeping her tod-dlers from running amok.

Scully did not mind the interruption. The direc-tion in which Mulder was taking the conversation made her uncomfortable.

"Thank you," the woman said, returning the pen.

"Don't mention it," Scully said.

"For the sake of discussion, let's say he did get sick last night," Mulder said, refusing to abandon the subject. When Mulder got hold of an idea, he was like a dog with a bone.

"What are you suggesting?" said Scully as they picked up their bags and headed for the departure gate. "That Gulf War Syndrome is caused by UFOs?"

"UFOs are frequently witnessed by soldiers in wartime," said Mulder.

Scully shook her head. "The only UFOs soldiers are likely to see are secret military aircraft."

They showed their tickets to a flight attendant and walked onto the plane.

By now Mulder had come up with a new theory. "What if that's what made the soldiers in Iraq sick? The exhaust or fuel of a classified aircraft or its weapon?"

Scully thought about it.

"There is a high-security air force base near Little Rock," she said. "There is a possibility that they could have been flying an experimental craft over Tennessee last night."

"They'd deny it, of course," said Mulder as he followed Scully down the narrow plane aisle to their seats. After they buckled themselves in, he continued, "But it could possibly explain how Ranheim developed those symptoms."

"Possibly," Scully reluctantly agreed. "The idea's worth pursuing, anyway. At least it's a more promising theory than UFOs."

"Right," said Mulder. "I know you like your explanations down-to-earth, Agent Scully." Then he smiled. "When we land in Washington, I know some people we can talk to about this."

"The military won't discuss a classified aircraft," said Scully. "Neither will anyone else in government."

"These people aren't in government," Mulder said. "They're out of it."

He grinned.

"Far out," he said.

At the Washington airport they grabbed a taxi. Mulder gave the driver an address in the heart of the city.

The street the cab took them to was in easy walking distance of the White House, but it could have been a world away. Idle men hung out on the sidewalks. Storefronts were boarded up. Most of the streetlights were broken, but the red neon sign of a noisy bar flashed on and off, on and off. A sense of menace hung like haze in the night air.

Mulder led Scully to a run-down office building with a steel door. He pressed the buzzer in a code-like series of long and short buzzes. After a minute an answering buzz let them in.

"Your friends seem to value security," said Scully.

"They have suspicious natures," agreed Mulder.

"So tell me, who are they?" Scully asked as the creaking elevator slowly rose.

"They consider themselves watchdogs for the public against government misdeeds," said Mulder. "They publish a magazine called *The Lone Gunman*. Some of their information is definitely first-rate.

Covert actions. Classified weapons. On the other hand, some of their ideas can easily be called weird."

The elevator came to a stop, and the doors slid open. Mulder led Scully down a grimy hallway to another steel door. Pasted on it was a poster from World War II that read: LOOSE LIPS SINK SHIPS. THE WALLS HAVE EARS.

"No need to knock," Mulder said.

Scully followed his gaze upward. Above the door, a TV eye watched them.

The door swung open. A medium-sized man in his thirties stood there, wearing a Ramones T-shirt, ancient Levi's, and ratty tennis shoes. His eyes gleamed behind black-framed glasses.

"Hi, Langly," Mulder said.

Langly didn't waste time saying hello.

"Guess who I had breakfast with last week?" he said. "The guy that shot John F. Kennedy."

Chapter SIX

"That so?" Mulder didn't bat an eye as Langly led them into the room.

"He's an old dude now," Langly said. "But yeah, he was dressed as a cop on the grassy knoll. No doubt about it. I got his testimony on videotape. Dynamite stuff."

"Shame Oliver Stone didn't use you when he made that movie," said Mulder.

"Who says he didn't?" Langly replied.

Scully looked around. The Lone Gunman's office was a cross between a high-tech showroom and a garage sale. Computers, fax machines, copiers, and gadgets were arrayed on tables stained by decades of coffee mugs and ancient markings from the days of pen and ink. The other two Lone Gunmen lounged on creaking swivel chairs, regarding her silently.

"Gentlemen, let me introduce my partner, Special Agent Dana Scully," Mulder said. "Scully, these gentlemen are—"

One of them, in a dark business suit, white shirt, and striped tie, interrupted, "Mulder, listen to this. You know Vladimir Zhirinovsky, the nationalist leader of the Russian Social Democrats? The mad dog who wants to start the Cold War back up?"

"The name sounds familiar," said Mulder.

"He's being put into power by the most evil force of the twentieth century," the man declared.

"Barney the dinosaur?" said Mulder.

The man chuckled despite himself. Then he turned grim again.

"The CIA," he said.

Now Scully tried not to smile.

The man turned to her.

"You don't believe it?" he said. "Well, that's to be expected, working as you do in the belly of the beast."

Mulder cut in smoothly. "Scully, this is Byers."

"Pleased to meet you," Scully said, extending her hand.

Byers ignored it. "So this is your partner," he said to Mulder. "I can see why you told us she was a skeptic."

Scully shot Mulder an accusing glare.

Mulder cleared his throat. "I merely said she was still inexperienced in certain areas."

"Thanks a lot, partner," Scully said.

"Time for you to be educated," Byers told her. "You don't believe that the CIA faces a loss of power and funding because of the end of the Cold War?

You don't think they want to have their old enemy back?"

"You give the government too much credit," Scully said.

The phone rang.

Byers turned on a tape recorder attached to the phone. He screwed a voice-masking device onto the mouthpiece.

"Lone Gunman," he said, picking up the phone.

He listened a moment, then put the phone down.

"They hung up," he said. He did not seem surprised. He turned back to Scully. "You were saying?"

"The government can't control the deficit or manage crime," Scully said. "What makes you think they can plan and execute such an elaborate conspiracy?"

"Hey, she's hot," said the third member of the staff. "Sharp and sweet—just the way I like 'em."

Scully gave the guy a look. He wore faded army fatigues with all insignia cut off and a Marine Corps–issue watch on his wrist. He leaned back in his swivel chair, Doc Marten boots propped on his desk, and returned Scully's look.

"Meet Frohike," said Mulder.

"*Pleased* to meet you," Frohike said. His gaze did more than take Scully in. It gobbled her up.

Scully was only too happy to turn back to Byers

as he went on. "We're not talking about the clowns performing for the media on Capitol Hill. We're talking about a dark network. A government within a government. A power we never see that controls our every move."

"How could they do that?" asked Scully.

"How?" Byers said, smiling. "I'll show you one way. Got a twenty?"

Scully took a twenty-dollar bill from her wallet. Byers grabbed it out of her hand. Before she could stop him, he tore a piece off the left side.

"*Hey*," Scully said.

Byers paid no attention. He concentrated on removing a thin plastic strip inside the bill.

"Take a look," he said triumphantly. "This magnetic strip lets them track you. When you pass through a metal detector at the airport, they know exactly how much money you're carrying and where you're carrying it to."

He handed the two parts of the bill back to Scully.

"Byers, I'm shocked," Mulder said, keeping a straight face. "You know it's a federal crime to deface money."

"That strip is to stop counterfeiting," Scully added.

"Then why is it on the inside?" Langly demanded.

"Other countries put it on the outside of the bill. What is being hidden?"

"Look, I hate to interrupt your train of thought," Mulder said. "But it's taking us off the track. It's not what I'm here for."

"Which is?" Byers said.

"Information," Mulder said.

"Of course," Langly said. "We're the only place to get the real stuff."

"Anything you and your lovely partner want," Frohike said.

"What do you people know about Gulf War Syndrome?" Mulder asked.

"It's the Agent Orange of the nineties," Langly said flatly.

"Comes from artillery shells coated with depleted uranium," added Byers.

"Do you know of any classified planes that were used in the Gulf War?" asked Mulder.

"Why expose a secret plane to the Iraqi Air Force? Those guys ran for cover whenever anything came near them," Byers said. "The answer is no."

Mulder moved on. "Any reports of UFO activity during that period?"

All three men broke into laughter.

"UFOs caused Gulf War Syndrome," said Langly, still chuckling. "That's a good one."

Byers patted Mulder affectionately on the shoulder. "That's why we like you, Mulder. Your ideas are even weirder than ours."

"It's good to know our national security is in your hands," agreed Langly.

"And those of your lovely partner," said Frohike. He got up from his chair and went to Scully. "Let's discuss threats to the country over coffee sometime. Anytime."

"Sorry, but my schedule's kind of full," she said, backing toward the door.

"Bring her around again," Frohike said to Mulder.

"I'll do that," Mulder said. "I'm sure I couldn't keep her away if I wanted to."

He turned to hear what Scully had to say.

But she was already out the door.

She stayed tight-lipped on the taxi ride to FBI Headquarters. Mulder had to wait until they were back in their office to hear her opinion of his friends.

"Those were the most paranoid people I have ever met," she told him, shaking her head. "I can't see how you can believe a word they say," she added as she began writing her report.

Mulder looked up from photos of the site of the truck accident. "I can't see how you can be so down on them—when they admire you so."

"Thanks, but no thanks," Scully said. Then she said, "Darn. This pen is out of ink."

As she unscrewed the pen to put in a new ink cartridge, she went on. "Mulder, didn't you see how they answered the telephone? They think every call they get is tapped. They're sure they're being followed everywhere they go. They are wacko. They actually believe that what they're doing is important enough for someone to—"

Scully froze.

"What's the matter?" asked Mulder.

Scully put her finger to her lips. Then she gestured for Mulder to come to her desk. She pointed at her pen.

A tiny chip was imbedded in it.

Scully didn't have to tell Mulder what it was. He had seen micro-listening devices before.

He remembered the mother at the airport who had borrowed the pen.

She had been too ordinary-looking to be true, he supposed.

He knew what the Lone Gunmen would say.

It was all normal—as normal as Mom and apple pie.

Chapter SEVEN

Mulder had lain in bed for hours. Then he had gotten up and paced his darkened apartment. In his mind he went over and over the sightings in Tennessee and what had happened afterward. He thought about the truck driver and the story of the encounter, which kept changing in the telling. And the police chief who didn't act like a chief but like a tool of higher-ups. And the bugging device in Scully's pen.

How did all of these puzzling pieces fit together?

What piece was missing?

There was only one way Mulder could think of to find it.

There was only one person Mulder knew who might have it.

Mulder didn't know his name. All Mulder had was a code name: Deep Throat.

Who was Deep Throat? What game was he playing with Mulder? That was another puzzle Mulder couldn't solve. Even trying to solve it would have broken one of the rules of Deep Throat's game. Mulder had to follow them all. For Mulder could be sure that this man who knew everything would know if Mulder ever cheated.

Following the rules, Mulder went to the desk lamp by the window. He unscrewed the clear lightbulb and screwed in a black one. He lifted his window blinds, switched on the lamp, and turned it so that the purple light shined outward into the night like an SOS beacon.

It was up to Deep Throat to see it and decide if he wanted to come to the rescue.

Mulder lay down on the couch to take a nap while Deep Throat made up his mind.

It seemed like he had just shut his eyes when the phone rang.

Instantly awake, nerves jangling, Mulder picked up the phone before it could ring twice.

He heard a series of clicks in clusters. He counted them silently, scribbling numbers on a notepad. After the last click came the humming of a phone hung up. Mulder glanced over the numbers he had scrawled. They told him where Deep Throat would show up and when. Then he went to his shredder and fed it the piece of paper and the one beneath. That was another of Deep Throat's rules. When it came to security, Deep Throat made the Lone Gunmen seem as trusting as Goldilocks.

☠ ☠ ☠

An hour later, in the deep darkness just before dawn, when the stars and the moon had disappeared, Mulder stood by the Potomac River below the Jefferson Memorial.

He looked up at the ghostly white dome. In his mind he recited the words carved into the stone. They came from the Declaration of Independence, which Thomas Jefferson had written two hundred-odd years ago. They said that men were born with the right to life, liberty, and the pursuit of happiness. And that governments got their power from the consent of the governed.

Mulder gazed at the river, whose ripples sparkled with reflected lights. His mouth curved in a thin smile. *A lot of water had gone down the river since those words had been written*, he thought.

Then he saw the reflection. A man was standing on the riverbank, less than five feet away.

The man had his overcoat collar turned up around a muffler that masked his lower face. His hat brim shaded his eyes. As Mulder turned, the man glided away to stand in shadow.

"Cold out." Deep Throat's voice, though low, moved like an arrow through the distance between them.

"It's still winter," said Mulder.

"Pitchers and catchers report for spring training next week."

"Yeah," Mulder said. Then, more sharply, "What are we doing here?"

"Always in a hurry, Mulder," he said dryly. "You have to learn patience to succeed in your calling. Now where were we?"

"At the ball game."

"Ah, yes," Deep Throat said. "Maybe this year we can catch a game. Of course, we wouldn't be able to sit together."

"Too bad," said Mulder. "Something tells me you have the connections to get great seats."

"At any park in the country," Deep Throat assured him. Then he stiffened.

A man, far down the riverbank, was snapping pictures of landmarks.

Mulder looked at Deep Throat.

He was standing like a deer frozen by a snapping twig or a strange scent.

"It's just a tourist," Mulder said.

Deep Throat didn't answer until the man lowered his camera and moved away. Then he said, "In our business, nothing is 'just' what it seems."

Mulder could hold back no longer. "Look, tell me, what am I onto?" he whispered urgently.

Deep Throat said nothing.

"We investigate a truck driver's encounter with a possible UFO," Mulder said. "He's sprung from custody before we can question him. Next thing we know, we're being bugged by highly sophisticated devices. Who is listening to us? And why?"

Deep Throat answered with silence.

"Why won't you tell me?" Mulder demanded.

Without a word, Deep Throat reached into his overcoat pocket. He pulled out a folded manila envelope and held it out to Mulder.

As Mulder took it, he saw Deep Throat raise his chin, about to say something.

But he did not. Instead, he turned and started to walk away.

"What am I onto?" Mulder asked again before Deep Throat could get out of earshot.

Deep Throat paused only long enough to toss a final crumb of information over his shoulder.

"A dangerous path," he told Mulder, in a voice as chilling as an owl's hooting in the dark.

Chapter EIGHT

Mulder was in his FBI office. It was morning, and he still had had no sleep. He rubbed his red-rimmed eyes. Then he plunged back into the report on his desk. The report came from the envelope Deep Throat had handed him. Mulder had gone over it endlessly, trying to take in all that it could possibly mean.

He was staring once again at the heading, "INTERCEPTED IRAQI TRANSMISSION," when Scully came in.

Mulder didn't bother looking up—until Scully tossed a report of her own onto his desk.

She saved him the trouble of reading it. "The truck was phony," she said, her voice snapping like a whip. "So was the truck driver, Ranheim."

"Your evidence?" said Mulder.

"First I checked the papers listing the contents of the truck," Scully said. "It said the truck was carrying a hundred and eight cartons of auto parts, bringing its total weight to thirty-one hundred pounds. I then checked three state highway weighing stations along his route. They all recorded the truck at fifty-one hundred pounds. Something is on that truck, and it's not auto parts."

"The weighing stations did not report the discrepancy, as required by law?" said Mulder.

"What do you think?" said Scully with a crooked smile.

"Considering what we already know about this case, I think you had to dig it out of them," Mulder said.

"You think right," said Scully.

"It all fits together," said Mulder.

Grimly, Scully went on. "And that's not all. Ranheim lied about being in the Gulf War, though I had to twist a few arms to find out the truth. His real name is Frank Druce, and he was in Special Operations, a Black Beret, in Mosul, northern Iraq."

Mulder's eyes flicked back to the heading of Deep Throat's report.

One word jumped out from it.

Iraqi.

"Go on," he said to Scully.

"Also, the other night's encounter wasn't what made Frank Druce sick," she said. "He's been to the military hospital for treatment three times this year. For an undisclosed illness—since Gulf War Syndrome doesn't officially exist."

Mulder had heard enough. Angrily he slammed his hand down on Deep Throat's report.

"We had it," he said in a pained voice. "We had it and we let it go."

"Had what?" said Scully. "Let it go where?"

"Four days ago, an Iraqi Air Force pilot shot down an unidentified flying object," said Mulder. "The wreckage, and possibly the occupants, were recovered by U.S. Army personnel near the northern Iraqi border. Ranheim, or I should say Druce, would be a perfect person to go over and escort whatever— or whomever—they found from the crash site—to a lab in the United States."

"That would explain why the truck weighs so much more than listed," said Scully. "But still it's hard to imagine that the army would—"

"The military has in the past transported dangerous materials and weapons in unmarked trucks across the country," Mulder cut in.

He saw Scully looking at him with lifted eyebrows.

He grinned at her and said, "I guess I'm starting to sound like the Lone Gunmen."

"The thought did cross my mind," Scully said.

Then she picked up Deep Throat's report.

A speed-reader, she flipped the pages to the end, then stared hard at Mulder.

"Where did you get this?"

Mulder did not meet her eyes.

"Let's just say it's a source—a source with deep background," he said.

"I want to know all about him," Scully said.

"I'd like to, too," Mulder said. "But all I know is that, on several occasions, he's guided us away from harm and pointed us in the right direction. He's our friend."

"You can't be sure of that," Scully insisted. "We work for the FBI and *we're* being bugged. What does that tell you?"

Mulder heard a note of mingled fear and anger in her voice. He remembered Scully when she had first become his partner. She'd believed what they had taught her at the FBI Academy. She'd really thought there was a sharp line separating the good guys from the bad. She'd imagined it was easy to tell them apart.

"Maybe it tells us that everything is not what it appears to be," he told her.

"Exactly," Scully said. "For all we know, this man with a deep background is deeply into bugging us. You said yourself you know next to nothing about him."

She took her pen out of her pocket and dropped it on the desk like a dead rat.

"I do know he's never lied to me yet," said Mulder.

"The operative word is *yet*," Scully said.

"I won't betray his confidence. I trust him."

"Mulder," Scully said, "*you're* the only one I trust."

"Then you'll have to trust me on this," he said.

She gave him a weak smile. "Do I have a choice?" she said. "Okay, lead on. What's next?"

"Did you find out where the truck is now?" Mulder asked.

Scully nodded. "I have a general picture. It's heading west, toward Colorado. Possibly in the direction of a high-security military base there."

"We have to intercept it," said Mulder. "We have to find out what's onboard. At the rate it's traveling, we should wrap up loose ends here at Headquarters, pick up stuff at our apartments, and head out before midnight."

"I hope you know what you're doing—trusting your deep connection," said Scully.

"I hope so, too," Mulder said. "But there's only one way to find out for sure."

Chapter NINE

That night, as Mulder unlocked his door, he sensed that something was wrong.

He was right.

When he closed the door and snapped the light switch on, he was sure of it.

The room stayed dark. The only light came from a streetlamp outside the window.

A voice came from an easy chair in Mulder's living room.

"I cut the main breaker," Deep Throat said.

Mulder could see his dim shape in the chair, his topcoat with the collar still turned up, his hat still on his head.

"You risk exposure coming here," Mulder said. "My apartment may be under observation."

"I am not unaware of that possibility," said Deep Throat dryly. "I have taken precautions. I have a certain experience in the area of security."

"I imagine so," Mulder said. "But still a risk remains."

"I have to take it," Deep Throat said. "The information I have to give you is too important."

Deep Throat tossed an envelope onto the coffee table.

"The photograph inside was taken by an officer at Fort Benning, Georgia," Deep Throat said. "Recently in that area, seventeen UFOs were reported in one hour."

"Is that where the Iraqi wreckage is being held?" Mulder asked. "Are UFOs tracking it?"

Deep Throat stood up.

"Nice place you have here," he commented as he headed for the door.

"Wait," Mulder said.

Deep Throat paused, hand on the doorknob.

"I . . . ," Mulder said, and stopped, even though questions were crowding his mind.

"Yes?" said Deep Throat.

Mulder sighed. He knew the rules. Deep Throat had said all that he was going to say.

"I . . . I have never had a chance just to thank you," said Mulder. "You've helped my work so much—without asking anything in return."

Deep Throat turned away as if he did not want to look Mulder in the eye.

"Do not presume to know my agenda," he said.

"You're right," Mulder said. "I'm in the dark about who you are, where you come from, what you want. But I do know you've put yourself at great risk to help me. So thank you."

Deep Throat glanced at Mulder. Then, without a smile or any acknowledgment, he was out the door, leaving Mulder alone with the envelope.

A half hour later, Mulder was with Scully. Side by side they stood looking down at a photograph that lay on her kitchen table.

"This was taken at Fort Benning, Georgia," Mulder said.

"Amazing," said Scully. "Of course, photographs can be doctored. They can lie."

"Let us proceed on the assumption that this one does not," said Mulder, his eyes unable to leave the image before them.

The photo, shot in the evening, was in color. In the darkening air hovered two circular craft. Each had a small upper deck above the main fuselage, with three blazing red lights forming a triangle beneath. On the ground two soldiers stood near a military station wagon. One of them was pointing up at the two craft. Near their feet was a puddle of water, evidently from a recent downpour.

"There were thunderstorms the night of the truck encounter," mused Scully.

Mulder was barely listening.

"It's the best photographic evidence I've ever seen," Mulder said, talking as much to himself as to his partner. He began pacing the kitchen. "When I saw the Gulf Breeze UFO photos, I knew they were a hoax. But this one—this one is a perfect example of the kind of positive evidence that the government has amassed for decades and kept secret."

As Mulder kept pacing and talking, Scully went to a drawer and pulled out a magnifying glass. With it, she bent over the photo.

"The whole business with the truck was a decoy," said Mulder. "It was designed to lead anyone hunting the UFO remains away from Fort Benning. It certainly fooled us. We were all set to head out West."

Scully said nothing. She was busy going over the photo with her magnifying glass.

"We have to leave immediately for Georgia," Mulder said. "We have to—"

Scully, straightening up, cut him off. "This photo is a fake," she said.

Mulder froze in his tracks.

Scully held the magnifying glass out to him. He took it.

He examined the photo while Scully pointed out, "The soldier's shadow is supposed to be caused by the light from the UFO. However, it falls in the wrong direction for that."

"There may be an off-camera light source creating that shadow," Mulder said.

"Look closely at the color of the reflected light on the station wagon windshield," Scully commanded.

Mulder did as directed.

"The reflection is from the red lights of the UFO," Scully said, her voice still cold. "But the color doesn't match those lights."

"Come on, Scully," Mulder said, still bent over the photo, turning his head to look up at his partner. "There's probably a degree of tint in the windshield. Or maybe the difference was caused by atmospheric conditions, car exhaust, jet pollution, a thousand things. Who knows?"

"We should have the photo analyzed," Scully said.

"Why not just say it, Scully," Mulder snapped. "You are determined not to believe him."

"Maybe you're *too* determined to believe him," Scully replied.

"I want to follow a lead that may result in real proof of extraterrestrial biological entities—E.B.E.'s." Mulder picked up the photo from the table and put it into his breast pocket.

"E.B.E.'s," he repeated softly. "I *need* to go to Fort Benning."

He started out of the kitchen, but Scully caught him by the sleeve. "Listen up, Mulder, just for a moment, *please*."

"Okay, I'm listening," he said.

"I have never known anyone so dedicated to and passionate about a belief as you," Scully said.

"Am I being complimented—or condemned?" Mulder asked.

"Your belief is so intense, it can be *blinding*," Scully said.

"What are you saying?" Mulder asked.

"There are others who know what I do about your passion," Scully said. "I respect and admire it. But those others will use it—against you."

Mulder said nothing. His face was blank.

"The truth is out there, Mulder," said Scully, making a last effort to break through the wall suddenly between them. "But so are lies."

Mulder didn't bother answering her.

He simply turned and left.

Chapter TEN

Scully did not try to go after Mulder. Her shoulders slumped when she heard her apartment door slam behind him. Shaking her head, she stared at the bare tabletop where the photo had lain.

She should have known that Mulder would not listen to her. Scully sighed. Mulder had taught her so much. Why wouldn't he let her teach him anything? Why wouldn't he listen to the voice of reason? His stubbornness should have made her angry. But it didn't. It made her sad. Sad that there was no way she could stop Mulder from going on what she thought was most probably a fool's errand. And sad that she hadn't had the quickness of mind to go with him, blind alley or not.

Scully was still glum when she rose the next morning at dawn, after a sleepless night, and went to work. The sky over Washington was gray with the threat of rain, and it matched her mood. Her feet were dragging as she walked down the corridors of FBI Headquarters toward the office she and Mulder shared.

She opened the office door. Suddenly her eyes

narrowed. She realized that Mulder's desk light was on.

Mulder was capable of leaving lights on, but she wasn't. And she had been the last one to leave the office yesterday.

Scully's mouth tightened. The people who had planted the bugging device in her pen wanted to do still more spying. And they could break into FBI Headquarters to do it.

Unless, of course, they didn't have to break in. Unless they were on the inside already.

Anything was possible, thought Scully. Nothing could surprise her anymore. The only thing surprising now was the light's being left on. They were getting sloppy. Unless, of course, she had surprised them by showing up so early.

Unless they were still—

She heard a sound behind her, and her hand flew to her purse, groping for her gun.

"I've been here all night," said Mulder.

Scully went limp.

"You shouldn't sneak up on people, Agent Mulder," she said. "The world is scary enough."

"Scarier and scarier," Mulder agreed as he laid out a series of photos on his desk. "I've had the photo analyzed by the Bureau's computers."

"And you found?" asked Scully. The original Fort

Benning photo was there, as well as a number of enlargements.

"At first the photo appeared genuine," Mulder said. "With no apparent signs of tampering. The film grain was the same throughout. So were the color levels and shading. Then I noticed this."

He pointed to the evening sky shown in the original photo. "Here's the moon," he said. "It's *half* full."

Then he pointed to the rain puddle in the photo. "As you see, there seems to be a faint reflection in the water. I made the puddle twenty-five times larger."

He pointed to the enlargement. "There's the reflection of the moon," he said. "But it's *one-quarter* full."

Mulder turned away from the photos. He stared off into space, his face hard. "Not to mention the fact that the water couldn't catch the moon's image from the angle shown. You were right, Scully. The photo is a fake."

Scully kept looking at it. "A very skillful fake," she said. "A fake that would have fooled almost anyone. A fake conceived by someone highly accomplished in the art of deception. In a way, it's a masterpiece of that art."

"But a fake nonetheless," said Mulder, his voice bleak. "He tried to deceive us."

Scully said nothing.

Mulder looked at her. "We're alone on this," he said. "There is no one we can trust now. They went to a lot of trouble to put us on the wrong track. But at least they wound up giving us one vital piece of information. One thing we can be certain of now."

"Which is?" asked Scully.

"There's something out there that no one is supposed to find," Mulder said.

"There's something else we can say for sure," Scully said.

"What's that?" asked Mulder.

"Someone out there will do anything in the world to keep us from finding it," Scully said.

Chapter ELEVEN

The best defense was a good offense, Mulder decided. That night he flashed Deep Throat another signal from his window.

This time the phone rang instantly. Mulder picked up the receiver and counted off the ticks.

Despite himself, he had to smile when he learned the meeting place.

The next morning Mulder stood watching gaudy tropical fish swim by behind thick glass in the Washington Aquarium. The tanks were brightly lit and the viewing areas kept dim, the better to see the underwater sights.

Mulder had been standing there for less than ten minutes when he saw the reflection beside him.

Again Deep Throat had his overcoat collar up and his hat brim down. Still, even in the glass, Mulder could see Deep Throat's eyes glowing intensely. Mulder did not turn to look at his neighbor. He merely shifted his gaze so that his mirrored eyes met Deep Throat's.

For a moment both men stood in silence, both refusing to blink.

Then Deep Throat demanded, "Why didn't you leave for Fort Benning?"

Mulder paused for a heartbeat to get his anger under control. Then he said flatly, "The photograph was a fake."

Deep Throat said nothing.

"At least you're not insulting my intelligence by pretending to be shocked at the news," Mulder said.

"On the contrary, I can only give you my compliments," Deep Throat declared. "The photo was prepared by people I consider the best in the business."

Mulder could restrain his anger no longer. "I thought you were an ally. I even thought you were a friend," he said bitterly.

"Oh, I am," Deep Throat said in a hurt tone. "I most certainly am."

"Run that past me again, would you," said Mulder. "With friends like you, I don't need—"

"Let me remind you," Deep Throat interrupted, "I place my life in danger every time we speak."

"Tell me more."

"I can only tell you this," said Deep Throat. "I have been a party to terrible lies told to the American people. I have seen deeds that even the most crazed mind could not imagine."

Deep Throat's eyes no longer met Mulder's in the

glass. Deep Throat was staring straight ahead, at creatures of the deep gliding by.

"I have spent years watching you, Agent Mulder, from my . . . lofty position," Deep Throat went on. "It has taken me years to decide you were the one I could trust."

"Then why did you lie to me?" Mulder demanded.

"I needed to divert you," Deep Throat said. "You and Agent Scully are fine investigators. And your motives are good. But there still are secrets that should remain secrets—truths that people are not ready to know."

"Who are you to decide that?" Mulder demanded.

"The reaction to such secrets would be too dangerous," Deep Throat declared.

"Dangerous?" said Mulder. "Dangerous in what way? Dangerous like people outraged by lies? Lies about the Kennedy assassination? MIAs? Radiation experiments on dying patients? Iran-Contra, Watergate, the Tuskegee experiments? When you start covering up things, where does it end? *Does* it end? Or with men like you in charge, does it keep on going on forever until the cover-up is everywhere and truth is nowhere to be found?"

Deep Throat was silent, still staring ahead.

"The transcript you gave me, of the Iraqi pilot," Mulder said. "That *is* the truth, isn't it?"

Deep Throat nodded.

"Then why did you even bother to show it to me?" Mulder asked.

"I was aware that you had learned about the truck and the sightings," Deep Throat said. "So I knew that, down the road, I would have to steer you away from what you should not know. I would have to lie to you, and my lie would have to be a good one. As I am sure you know, Agent Mulder, a lie is easiest to swallow when it is sandwiched between two truths."

"Is that all you have to say?" asked Mulder.

Deep Throat's silence was his answer.

"Thanks—for nothing," Mulder said with disgust, and started to walk away.

"Mulder," said Deep Throat.

Mulder turned back to look at Deep Throat in the glass.

"Mulder," Deep Throat said, "if a shark stops swimming it will die."

He paused, like a tired runner taking a deep breath. "Mulder, don't stop swimming."

He had only one more thing to say before he turned and wearily walked away.

"I am not responsible for the electronic surveillance, Mulder. But I do know they can still hear you."

Chapter TWELVE

The first thing Mulder did when he got home after leaving Deep Throat was to take down every framed picture from every wall in his apartment.

After that he started on the rest of his home, working with passionate intensity.

In the kitchen he looked under the counters, took apart every appliance, emptied every drawer.

In the bathroom he checked the faucets, the shower head, and the toilet, and unscrewed the pipes.

In the living room he turned furniture upside down, dismantled the TV and VCR, unzipped cushions, unscrewed lightbulbs, even checked out his telephone, though he suspected that would be too obvious.

He was just unscrewing a switchplate in his bedroom when the doorbell rang.

He went to the front door and opened it.

It was Scully.

"Glad to see you," he said.

"What were you doing, working out?" she asked, seeing his shirt drenched with sweat.

Then Scully looked at his apartment turned upside down.

"Mulder, what has—?" she started to ask.

Mulder put his finger to his lips, and Scully shut her mouth.

Silently he led her to the bedroom.

As Scully watched, he finished unscrewing the switchplate. His face lit up, but only for a moment. Then it darkened with anger. He pointed to a tiny chip attached to the wires behind the plate. He didn't have to tell Scully what it was.

Mulder gave it one last glare. Then he strode to the living room, with Scully following.

Again he gestured for her to be silent.

"I've been doing a lot of thinking about this whole situation," he said as he sat down by a laptop computer on his coffee table.

Meanwhile Scully's eyes were darting around the ruins of the room. By now she understood what had happened to it. Her mouth was grim.

"They've won this one," said Mulder. "Let's just move on."

He started typing on the laptop.

Scully watched his message scroll out letter by letter on the screen:

"WE HAVE TO FIND THE TRUCK."

Scully met his eyes and silently nodded.

☠ ☠ ☠

Without a word, Mulder pointed at the rearview mirror of his car. He was driving down Pennsylvania Avenue in the heart of Washington with Scully beside him. She looked in the mirror and saw that the black sedan was still on their tail. It had been behind them ever since they'd left Mulder's apartment.

That was only to be expected, Scully thought. *The only good thing about these people was that they were so predictable.*

"Look, Scully, this isn't really part of our job," Mulder said in a loud, distinct voice. "I mean, no one has assigned it to us. If you don't want to go through with this, just get out and go right back to the office. I'll understand."

"I'm glad you feel that way," Scully said just as clearly. "Count me out. No hard feelings, I hope."

"Sure, no hard feelings," Mulder said.

He stopped by the curb, and Scully got out.

She watched Mulder drive off and then started walking quickly down a side street.

Glancing back, she saw a man jumping out of the black sedan to follow her, while the car started off after Mulder.

Those people might be predictable, she thought, but they were also smart.

Whether they had a bug in Mulder's car or not, they were covering all bases.

Scully spotted a taxi.

She hailed it and jumped into the backseat.

"Dulles Airport, fast," she told the cabbie. "An extra twenty if you bend the speed limit."

As the cab shot into high gear, she glanced out the back window.

The man from the black sedan was desperately looking for a cab. He was not having any luck.

Scully settled back in her seat.

From here on in, she suspected, the name of the game would be luck.

Chapter THIRTEEN

"Where to?" the young woman at the airline ticket counter asked.

"Round trip to Chicago," Scully said. "The next flight out."

Scully handed the clerk a credit card, and the clerk bent over her computer terminal to enter the card number and get the ticket.

Scully checked out the clerk as she clicked the keys. The clerk was pretty, blond, and bland. *She fit her role perfectly—maybe too perfectly,* Scully thought. If Scully had to choose an agent to work here, it would be just this type. And if Scully had to pick a spot to put an agent, it would be right here. What better place to keep an eye on where people went?

Come on, Scully, she told herself. *You're getting as bad as the Lone Gunmen. The invisible government isn't everywhere. It can't be.*

"There you are, Ms. Scully," the clerk said with a smile too bright to be real. "A round-trip ticket to Chicago. Here's your credit card. The plane departs at gate thirty-five."

"Thank you," Scully said, taking the ticket and her credit card. Then she said, "I'd also like a one-way ticket on the next flight to Los Angeles, with a stop in Las Vegas."

The clerk raised her eyebrows slightly, then quickly flashed another smile. "Yes, ma'am," she said. She punched out the request on her computer and told Scully the fare.

"Sorry, but there's no discount one-way," the clerk apologized.

"That's all right," Scully said. "It's business."

"Same credit card?" asked the clerk. "Or do you want to use a corporate one?"

"Neither," Scully said. "I'll pay cash."

Scully counted out the sum in twenties on the counter. The clerk stared at the bills as if she had never seen actual money before. Then she recounted the bills slowly, put them away awkwardly, and handed Scully the ticket.

As Scully watched the twenties going into the drawer, she remembered the demonstration with the magnetic strips at The Lone Gunman office. *Those guys couldn't be right,* she told herself. *Could they?*

If they were, currency could give away her movements as easily as credit cards. Which meant there was nowhere to hide from eyes watching her every move, no matter how fast she traveled or what tricks she used.

"The Los Angeles flight leaves in just half an hour at gate seventeen," the clerk said.

"Thank you," said Scully shortly, putting the ticket with the other one into her handbag and walking quickly away.

She could feel the clerk's eyes following her. The clerk's, and who else's?

Meanwhile, miles away, Mulder did not have to wonder if anyone was following him.

He could still see the black sedan in the rearview mirror as he headed out of Washington on the four-lane highway toward Baltimore.

Mulder saw a red light at an approaching inter-section. Slowing his car, he eased into the right lane, flashing his signal for a right turn.

In the mirror, he watched the black sedan do the same.

Just as Mulder reached the intersection, the light turned green—and Mulder violently swung the wheel to the left while pressing the accelerator to the floor.

Screeching, the car barreled across the path of drivers in the lane beside it and then drivers going in the other direction.

As his car completed the wild turn and sped down an almost empty stretch of highway, Mulder realized he had been holding his breath. Emptying his lungs and gulping fresh air, he looked in the mirror and saw a traffic jam at the intersection. The black sedan hadn't made it through.

As soon as Mulder was out of sight of the intersection, he swung onto a side road and started circling back toward Baltimore and its airport.

Four hours later, Mulder and Scully met at the Las Vegas Airport.

They didn't say hello, though. They didn't even look at each other.

They stood side by side at a magazine rack, each leafing through a magazine.

They spoke to each other with their eyes glued to the pages, raising their voices only enough to be heard above the jangle of nearby slot machines.

"I tied up an airphone on the plane for three hours," Mulder said. "I called every weigh station and Bureau office west of the Mississippi."

"Me too," Scully said. "My ear is numb from being stuck on hold."

"At least we can be sure they didn't trace our calls," Mulder said.

"Can we?" said Scully.

Mulder shrugged as he turned a page of his magazine. "We did our best, anyway. Problem is, though, I didn't find the truck. You have any luck?"

"Yep," Scully said, staring at a glossy picture of a model in a Paris fashion show. "The truck is heading northwest on I-90. We have to buy a ticket to Seattle."

Mulder stared at a photo of Michael Jordan in the air, the basketball leaving his hands. "The Pacific coast. End of the line," he said.

"Right," said Scully, closing her magazine and returning it to the rack. "One way or another."

Chapter FOURTEEN

At the Seattle airport, Mulder and Scully rented a car. They had to use a credit card. The rental agency refused to touch cash.

"Langly at The Lone Gunman claims that the government plans to stop printing money," Mulder said. "Everyone will have to use plastic. That way there'll be no way to hide how much you have and what you do with it."

"A while ago I would have called the idea crazy," Scully said.

"And now?" asked Mulder.

"Now I think we'd better check our car for bugs," said Scully.

By late afternoon they were parked among tall timber by the side of Interstate 90. Scully scanned passing traffic through binoculars while Mulder studied a map of the area.

"Think about it," Mulder mused. "That truck has driven all the way across America. Just an ordinary-looking truck, ignored by everyone. No one suspects it's hauling a spacecraft from another world."

"There's a lot of things nobody in the country suspects," said Scully. "Except, of course, a few nuts."

Suddenly she straightened in her seat, her eyes glued to the binoculars.

"Here we go," she said.

She handed Mulder the binoculars.

"That's our baby," Mulder agreed, focusing on the approaching truck.

Mulder put down the binoculars and turned on the ignition. He waited with the motor purring until the truck was past. He waited a few more seconds. Then he swung the car onto the highway and went after the truck, staying far enough behind not to look too suspicious but making sure to keep it in sight.

Dusk was falling when the truck turned off the highway onto a two-lane blacktop that wound through the forest. The truck dropped its speed, and so did Mulder.

"Looks like a road to nowhere," Mulder said as they crawled along.

"Want me to drive?" Scully suggested. "When we dip under forty, you start looking like a horse chomping on the bit."

"Good idea," said Mulder, pulling over.

Two hours later, all they could see of the truck was its taillights, shining before them in the dark of a moonless night.

"Mulder, we've been trailing this truck forever," Scully said. "Maybe he knows we're following him and is taking evasive action."

"That's a possibility," agreed Mulder. "On the other hand, he could be leading us into—"

That was as far as he got.

The world exploded in a blast of blinding white light.

The light blossomed like a gigantic flower in front of them and flooded the car.

With the light came a low humming that filled the night air.

Scully had swerved to the side of the road before she could slam on the brakes. A fierce wind blew a hail of leaves and twigs from the forest against the car windows. The car rocked as if pounded by a gigantic fist. The radio, turned on low, shot up in volume. Stations followed one another in an ear-splitting parade of programs.

Then, as suddenly as it had begun, it was over.

Scully and Mulder sat stunned in their car, surrounded by silence and night.

Mulder recovered first.

Cautiously he opened the car door and stepped outside. He looked up at the sky. He saw only scattered stars.

Then he looked at the truck. Its rear lights were still on. It had stopped, too, by the side of the road. Its dark shape was tilted, its right wheels off the asphalt.

Scully got out from behind the wheel to join him.

"You okay?" he asked her.

She nodded weakly, unable to speak. Her heart was still stuck in her throat.

Mulder patted her on the shoulder reassuringly. Then he reached into the car and pulled out a flashlight.

Scully followed as he headed for the truck. He went along its side to the driver's cabin. His flashlight beam showed the driver's door hanging open.

Mulder shined his flashlight inside.

No one was there.

There was only the sound of the radio turned on low, and the debris of food wrappers, Styrofoam coffee cups, and spare warm clothing scattered on the floor.

"Looks like there was some kind of struggle," said Scully, peering over Mulder's shoulder.

"Ranheim!" Mulder shouted into the night. "Are you around here?"

There was no answer.

"Come on," Mulder said to Scully. "It's show-and-tell time."

Mulder led the way to the back of the truck.

Both of them stared at the back doors. They were open a crack.

Mulder paused. He took a deep breath and exhaled. Then he pulled the doors all the way open.

Piled high in front of him were cartons labeled AUTO PARTS.

Mulder lifted one. It was light as a feather.

"Decoys, of course," he said, and tossed the empty box out the back. Scully reached in and did the same with another.

Through the gap a red light came pouring out.

Mulder and Scully squinted into that gap, their faces bathed in red light.

"Scully," was all Mulder could manage to say.

"Oh my God," she gasped, seeing what he saw.

Behind the wall of cartons was a thick panel of shatterproof glass. Behind that glass was a mobile hospital unit, lit by bright red light. Bathed in that light were medical instruments and life-support machines. There was a small bed as well, with a net instead of a mattress, like a hammock on a steel frame.

The bed was empty.

Mulder slowed his pounding heart enough to voice his thoughts.

"It *was* an extraterrestrial biological entity," he said. "An E.B.E. *Alive!*"

"Where is it now?" said Scully. "And Ranheim?"

Mulder's voice was awestruck. "I think we were just witness to a rescue mission."

He stared at the empty bed.

"A successful one," he said.

Chapter FIFTEEN

Scully saw Mulder's eyes shining in the eerie red light. He had the look of a man in a holy place.

"My God, Mulder," she told him, "I can't stop shaking." Then she saw his eyes cloud over.

"Mulder, what's wrong?" she asked.

"Nothing—maybe," Mulder said. "A thought just struck me."

"What was it?" Scully asked.

"Wait here," was all he would say.

Mulder went to their car. When he returned he was carrying a radiation detector, a tape measure, and a stopwatch.

Scully saw what was on his mind when he measured an area around the truck, then swept the ground with the detector.

"Our encounter—does it fit the profile?" she asked.

Mulder's voice was dry. "Are you trying to ask me if it was real? If we actually did have a close encounter?"

Scully could only nod.

Mulder looked at the stopwatch in his hand.

Then he pulled another stopwatch from his pocket. He compared the two readings.

"Any difference?" asked Scully.

"No," Mulder said shortly. He stared at the watches a moment longer, as if hoping that somehow he had read them wrong. Finally he turned to face Scully with stricken eyes. "It was another hoax."

"But—*how?*" Scully asked. "How could anyone generate such terrific force?"

"Whatever they used, we've probably never heard of it," Mulder said. "The billions spent on secret hardware haven't all been wasted. Imagine weapons utilizing ultrasound shock waves. And supersonic stealth helicopters with high-intensity lights. Anything you can imagine, they can have— and use." He shrugged. "It doesn't really matter what it was. What matters is that there is no evidence it was a UFO."

"You mean they went through this big phony show just to try to put us off the trail again?" said Scully.

"It would seem so," Mulder declared.

"But wouldn't it simply have been easier for them to . . . to . . ." Scully had trouble voicing the idea.

Mulder did it for her. "To kill us?" he said. "I wonder about that myself."

He gathered up his equipment, then said to Scully, "You were right once about them spotting my weakness and targeting it. You might be right again. They may have been using me against myself. They know how much I want to believe that a close encounter is possible. They could have counted on me taking this one at face value and walking away satisfied."

He and Scully slowly walked back to the car, leaving the empty truck like a deflated balloon behind them.

"Now we have nothing to go on," said Scully. "No one to turn to."

"There is one player in all of this who hasn't lied—not to my face at least," said Mulder.

"Who's that?" asked Scully.

"I couldn't tell you that even if I wanted to," said Mulder. "Anyway, he's not exactly someone we can turn to right now."

"We're on our own then," said Scully as she got behind the steering wheel.

"Well, we can always use a little help from our friends," Mulder said.

The next morning there was a knock on Mulder's motel room door.

"Come in—it's unlocked," he shouted.

It was Scully, carrying her laptop.

"Do you consider this proper security?" she asked as she closed the door behind her, then locked it.

"Considering whom we're up against, I don't believe a standard door lock offers significant protection," said Mulder.

"Point taken," Scully said.

Mulder was sitting on his bed. Maps and pieces of papers covered with scrawled calculations were spread out around him. Scully noted that the bed had not been slept in.

Mulder had a phone in his hand. He looked at a thick black personal phone book lying open on his lap and punched out a number.

"Nick?" he said. "This is Mulder. What's shaking?"

Mulder listened a few moments, then said, "Let's see if I've got it right. There was Leverling. And also Priest Rapids on the east bank of the Columbia River? Did you send a field investigator?"

Mulder nodded at the answer, then asked, "And you can definitely vouch for the sightings? Back them up with solid testimony?"

He nodded again and said, "Okay. Thanks a million, Nick." Mulder hung up the phone.

Picking up a map, he went to Scully, who had set up her laptop on a table. She had stayed awake all night herself, typing up a report on the case so far.

Now she sat poised to record the latest developments.

"I've contacted every organization that has hot lines for UFO sightings," Mulder told her. "The Center for UFO Studies in Chicago. MUFON. NICAP. All the others. They've never seen such activity in a one-week period."

Mulder showed Scully a map of the United States. On it was a trail of red marks from coast to coast.

"It starts in Tennessee, where Ranheim was encountered," he said. "It goes on from there."

Scully studied the map. "These alleged sightings do follow the probable path of the truck," she said.

"And look," Mulder said. "After last night's hoax, there were seven sightings in Mattawa, Washington. That's a hundred miles away. Our visitors from out there must be desperately seeking a way to get their colleague back."

"And you think, whoever they are, they've located the final destination of the captured E.B.E.?" Scully asked.

"I think they have," Mulder said. His finger came down on the map—to hit the seven red marks clustered around a single spot near the Oregon coast. "And so have we."

Chapter SIXTEEN

"This is nowheresville," said Scully. "A rural town. A few farms and orchards. A lot of second-growth wilderness. We've been driving around for hours and seen nothing."

"Nowheresville is precisely the place you'd want to put a high-security facility," said Mulder, peering out the car window as they went down a narrow road past an abandoned orchard and encroaching woodland.

"Well, we'll have to knock off soon," said Scully, steering the car carefully around potholes. "Sun set an hour ago. Whatever might be here is hidden in the dark."

"Then there's something else we can look for," Mulder said.

"What's that?" Scully asked.

"Lights in the sky," Mulder answered.

"Sure, Mulder," Scully said. "Sure."

Then, suddenly, her eyes widened. "Mulder, see what I do?" she asked.

"Hard to miss it," said Mulder.

The car had rounded a bend in the road. In the sky was a fiery glow.

"Go for it," Mulder said eagerly.

But he slumped back in his seat as they got closer and saw what the glow was.

"Somebody's set up lights up on that hilltop," said Scully. "The locals are having a party. I can hear music."

"I guess it's worth investigating," Mulder said, trying to keep the disappointment out of his voice. Leave no stone unturned."

"And no light ignored." Scully brought the car to a stop. "This is as far as the road goes. We'll have to walk the rest of the way."

Leaving the car, they found a path winding through low undergrowth up the hill. They followed it, moving cautiously.

As they neared the top, Scully could see perhaps two dozen men and women dancing to rock from a powerful boom box. The scene was lit by the yellow glow of Coleman lanterns.

"Looks like Halloween comes a little late out here," she said.

Most of the people were in costume. Some wore grotesque rubber alien masks. Others wore home-made space suits. Above them a banner hung from two tall poles. Red block letters spelled out a greeting: WELCOME SPACE BROTHERS.

"Hey, man, join the party," a voice boomed out. A

big, bearlike man wearing an alien mask walked toward Mulder. The name "Freddie" was stitched on his shirt pocket.

Then he turned to Scully. "Ahh-doo-nay-vah-so-barahgahs," he said.

"Huh?" Scully replied.

"That's a greeting in the intergalactic language we've developed. We hope to make it standard throughout the universe," Freddie explained.

"And it means?" Scully said.

" 'Hello, space brothers,' " Freddie told her.

"And sisters, too, I presume?"

"Uhh, right," said Freddie. "I'll make a note of that. We still have a few glitches to work out."

"So, tell me, what's going on here?" Scully asked as Mulder stood by, smiling.

"A UFO party," Freddie said. "We have cause to celebrate."

"You've seen UFOs here?" Mulder demanded.

"This very spot," Freddie said.

"You're sure of that?"

"Positively."

"When did the sightings occur?"

"The last two nights," said Freddie.

"Have you established communication with the visitors?" asked Mulder.

"Unfortunately, not yet," Freddie said. "But we

expect them to come again. They're drawn here by our electric power. They hover over the power plant down there."

"A power plant?" said Scully. "Here?"

"Of course," Freddie said. "The utility companies hide them away—so we don't see how much pollution they cause. But, hey, what the public doesn't know can't hurt them."

"Interesting," said Mulder. "I'd like to take a look at it."

"You won't be able to get a good look until daylight," said Freddie. "They keep their lights down low. As I said, it's a real low-profile operation." Freddie started dancing in place, snapping his fingers to the music. "Party with us, man. We want to show our brothers up there what a warm welcome awaits them."

Mulder smiled thinly. "I suspect they already know what to expect from earthlings," he said.

"You can dance till dawn, then check out the power station."

"Sorry," said Mulder. "Next time. Right now I want to take a look-see. I have night binoculars."

"Well, have it your way," said Freddie, shaking his spaceman head. "But, hey! Different strokes for different folks. You can get a clear view of the station from the other side of the hilltop."

As Freddie rejoined his friends, Mulder and Scully went to view the spot that had drawn the lights in the sky.

Mulder looked down the hill through his night glasses.

Silently he passed the binoculars to Scully.

"Whatever it is, it's high-tech—and high-security," Scully said, studying the large building below. It was made of poured concrete, with no windows and one steel door. The area around it was blacktopped and surrounded by a high electrified wire fence. Dozens of cars, Jeeps, and trucks were parked near the building, and two men guarded the gate. They wore no uniforms and carried no weapons. But from the way they held themselves, Scully had no doubt that the clothes they wore *were* uniforms, and that weapons could appear at any instant.

"I'd hate to disillusion Freddie, but that's no power station," Scully said, passing the glasses back to Mulder.

He put them to his eyes.

Then he stiffened as if a current had passed through him.

"Bingo!" he said.

Chapter SEVENTEEN

"It's him, I'm sure," said Mulder, still peering through the binoculars. Then he passed them to Scully. "You can confirm the ID."

Scully looked through the glasses. Several men in lumber jackets had come out of the building. One of them was the truck driver who had called himself Ranheim.

"We've done it," Mulder exulted. "We've found it!"

"I hate to be a wet blanket, Mulder," Scully said. "But before you start celebrating like your friends, there are a few minor details to consider."

"Like what?" As he looked down at the building Mulder's eyes were shining.

"We can safely assume that they have the tightest possible security at this facility," Scully said. "We're not talking locks we can pick or phony identity cards we can flash. We're talking the most advanced, state-of-the-art protection. As for our FBI shields, they'll be as much use as the badges you get in Cracker Jack boxes."

Mulder nodded. "Entry does pose a certain problem," he agreed. "However, where there's a problem, there's also a solution. Fortunately, we have friends who are deeply into solving problems concerning security. This is exactly the kind of challenge they're looking for."

"You're not talking about those Lone Gunman guys, are you?" Scully shook her head.

Mulder nodded. "Whatever your opinion of their belief system, you cannot deny they have a certain technical expertise."

Scully shrugged. "I guess it's worth a try."

Mulder already had his cellular phone out. He punched in a number with machine-gun rapidity.

"Langly, this is Mulder. Turn off your tape recorder," he said into the phone.

He waited until the voice on the other end reluctantly said, "Okay. It's off."

Mulder waited another moment, then said more loudly, "Turn it off!"

There was a loud sigh on the other end. Then, after another pause, Langly declared, "Okay, okay. It's *off*!"

"Langly, we would like you to hack Agent Scully and myself names and identification numbers that will pass through security at the highest government levels," Mulder said.

"You kidding, Mulder?" Langly said. "You know what that would entail? We would have to penetrate the national security computer system by breaking its latest access code. We would then have to work around the most recent roadblocks set up to deter unauthorized activity. Next we would have to alter the database without detection. After that we'd have to exit, leaving no trace of entry. I mean, much as we at The Lone Gunman like you, Mulder—"

Langly paused a moment, then went on, "Frohike has asked me to add that we are extremely fond of your very attractive partner as well. But we are right in the middle an urgent task and I'm afraid we're far too busy to—"

"Langly," Mulder cut in, "what would you say to the first totally authentic photo of an extraterrestrial biological entity?"

"No way," said Langly, and gave a whistle of awe. "A real live E.B.E.?"

"A real live E.B.E.," affirmed Mulder.

After a brief pause, they heard a babble of off-phone voices in The Lone Gunman's office.

Langly came back on the line. "Look, can you wait an hour for the stuff you want? Sorry for the delay, but one of our computers is down."

Exactly an hour and a quarter later, one of the guards walked to the rental car that had driven up to the electrified gate.

Mulder rolled down his window.

"Hi, folks," the guard said. "You lost out here? Be glad to direct you to the nearest town. There's also a motel a ways down the road."

"I'm Braidwood," said Mulder. "My partner here is Stefoff."

The guard nodded to his partner, who was listening with him. The partner produced a laptop from a backpack and tapped away.

He looked up and nodded.

"Personal identification number?" the first guard demanded.

"Seven five nine three," said Mulder.

"Eight two four seven," said Scully.

The guard looked at his partner again. The partner tapped out the numbers, then nodded.

"Open the trunk, please," the first guard commanded.

Mulder pressed the trunk release button on the dashboard.

He sat stiffly, hands white-knuckled on the steering wheel, staring straight ahead, listening to the guard rummaging through the trunk. Beside him Scully sat staring straight ahead as well, barely breathing.

"Okay," the guard said, swinging open the gate. "Park in lot four."

Mulder let the air out of his lungs. He took a deep breath and started the car.

But the car was only halfway through the gate when the second guard looked up from his computer and shouted, "Hey, you, *wait!*"

"Oh, God," Scully said in a voice that only Mulder could hear.

But Mulder had a hunch that nobody—not even the Lone Gunmen—could help them now.

Chapter EIGHTEEN

Mulder considered his options.

He could gun the car forward—but there was nowhere to go.

He could shift into reverse and try for a getaway. But that would end all chance of penetrating the facility.

He could reach for his gun, and Scully could do the same. But there was no chance of winning a firefight after the first shot sounded and more guards came pouring out of the building.

Or he could do what was left for him to do. He could sit and wait for the guard to reach the car and then play it by ear.

The seconds it took for the guard to arrive seemed like hours.

The guard's face was dark with anger when he arrived.

"What's the matter with you two?" he asked. "You forgot to take these."

Through the open car window he handed Mulder and Scully clip-on visitor passes.

"Yeah, right, sorry," said Mulder, clipping the pass on. "It was a long trip out here. I'm a little groggy."

"I know what you mean," said the guard, and waved them through the gate. "Remember, parking lot four."

"Sure," said Mulder. "I don't want to get towed away."

"It wouldn't be your car that was hauled," said the guard. "It would be you—feetfirst."

Mulder found the lot marked with a bright red 4 and parked in it.

He and Scully went to the steel front door and straightened their clip-on passes.

"Here we go," said Mulder, pulling the door open.

There was no one inside on guard.

"This is almost too easy," Mulder said as they walked down a deserted corridor.

He glanced into the offices that lined the corridor, where uniformed men and women sat working at their desks. No one looked up as the two visitors walked by.

"Level one . . . level two." Scully read signs posted in the corridor.

"Langly said there's a level six in this facility," said Mulder. "He couldn't get us clearance for it, though. It was the one access code he couldn't break."

"Why do I think that's where we want to go?" said Scully as they took the elevator to the second floor.

There they found levels three and four.

"Getting close," Mulder said.

"Up we go again," said Scully, pressing the elevator button.

"Level five," she read when the elevator let them off.

Mulder was already moving down the corridor, like a tiger scenting territory.

Scully followed close behind.

An MP stood in front of a large door, his hand on the butt of his holstered pistol. His eyes said he was ready to use it.

Mulder and Scully walked past him, chatting about the weather.

The marking on the door he guarded said LEVEL SIX—CLEARANCE AA ACCESS ONLY.

"So close," said Mulder, after they turned a corner of the corridor.

"And yet so far," said Scully. "That MP doesn't look like he's into small talk. Small arms is more like it."

"We have to get through that door," said Mulder fiercely.

"No way will that guard let us," said Scully.

"Let's just go past again," said Mulder. "Maybe we can spot another way in."

"That MP sees us a second time and he'll get suspicious," Scully cautioned.

But Mulder was already heading back.

Scully grimaced. She should have known better than to try to stop Mulder when he was so near to what he wanted so badly. Nothing would stop him. Nothing short of a gun.

The MP produced the gun when Mulder and Scully came back around the corridor corner.

He must have followed them and waited there, Scully realized with a sinking feeling.

He must have heard every word they said.

"You folks come with me," he told them.

"I'm sorry, we're just lost," Mulder said. "If you could just tell us—"

"You two move ahead of me down the hallway, hands well away from your sides," the MP instructed.

"We're agents of the Federal Bureau of Investigation," Scully said. "I'm reaching for my identification—"

"I said, *march*," the MP commanded.

"But—" said Mulder.

The MP loudly clicked off the safety on his big .45. "Do I make myself clear?" he said. "Let's go, *now*."

As Mulder and Scully obeyed, the MP reached for a radio mike clipped to his shoulder strap.

He spoke into it. "This is level six. I've got a male and female who've identified themselves as—"

At that moment they were passing the door marked LEVEL SIX.

Scully could almost hear something inside Mulder snap.

"Mulder, no!" she cried—too late.

Mulder was dashing for the door.

The MP was leveling his gun.

All Scully could do was leap in front of the gun as the MP screamed, "Stop!"

Chapter NINETEEN

The MP's finger froze on the trigger as Scully leaped in front of him.

That gave Mulder just enough time to open the door, dash inside, and close the door behind him.

As he locked it, the alarm bells started to ring. The lock would buy him time, he hoped. Not much. But maybe enough.

Enough time to see what he had been looking for so hard, so long. He had never had a chance like this before. He might never have it again.

With the door closed, Mulder was in a darkness lit only by dim green lights. After a moment his eyes adjusted enough for him to see that he was at the top of a metal stairwell. Swiftly he moved down the iron steps, his shoes clanging and echoing.

At the bottom of the stairwell was another door. It, too, was marked LEVEL SIX. Mulder took a deep breath. He pushed at it with the flat of his hand and felt it swing open.

Inside was a vast laboratory lit by violet and blue lights filled with enough experimental apparatus to outfit a spacecraft.

Mulder didn't pause to examine any of it, though. His eyes were fixed on the large glassed-in chamber at the far end of the lab.

Leading into the chamber were dozens of tubes and wires. Pulsing out of it was an eerie red light.

Mulder recognized it as a larger twin of the life-support unit he had seen in the back of the abandoned truck.

As he headed for it, he realized he was sweating.

"Stop right there!" a voice boomed behind him. His sweat turned cold.

He turned and stared into the barrels of three shotguns, all pointed at his head.

The three MPs who held them were backed by three others with drawn .45s.

"Don't move," said one of the MPs with a shotgun. Mulder could see his finger curled tensely around the trigger.

"Don't even think of moving," said a second MP. The look on his face dared Mulder to try.

Mulder knew there were some tight corners you could try to talk your way out of. But this didn't look like one.

"Let him go!" a voice commanded.

The soldiers made no move to lower their weapons.

"*Let him go!*" the voice repeated, thundering now.

Reluctantly the soldiers lowered their guns and

turned to face the man who had emerged from the side door of the lab.

He stood with his overcoat collar turned up. His face was hidden in the shadow of his pulled-down hat brim.

"You've done well, men," Deep Throat told the soldiers. "Dismissed."

A puzzled look passed over the MPs' faces. But they did not ask questions. They lowered their weapons and left the lab.

Mulder and Deep Throat faced each other. They were no more than twenty feet apart, but the distance between them had never seemed so vast. When they spoke, it was as if they spoke from separate worlds.

"I know how badly, how very badly, you would like to look through the window of that chamber," Deep Throat said.

As if answering that challenge, Mulder turned and started for the chamber again.

"It would be pointless," Deep Throat said, stopping Mulder in his tracks.

Mulder gave Deep Throat a look that was a silent question.

Deep Throat answered with a nod. "It's dead," he said, in a voice as chill and bleak as death.

"Dead?" Mulder tried to say. But his lips would not form the word.

He could only listen as Deep Throat went on. "After a similar incident in 1947, there was a conference of world powers to decide what to do in such cases. Though the Cold War had already begun, a perfect accord was reached among the United States, the Soviet Union, the People's Republic of China, Britain, both parts of divided Germany, and France."

"A similar incident?" said Mulder. "A conference? An international treaty? I've never heard of any of it. Not in all of my research."

"You wouldn't have," Deep Throat said. "It was ultrasecret—and has been kept so by people who know how to keep secrets well."

"I can believe that, " said Mulder. "Tell me, then, what kind of agreement was made."

"It was decided that if any extraterrestrial biological entity survived such a crash, the country that captured the E.B.E. would be responsible for it."

"Responsible for it?" said Mulder.

"I should say, responsible for its—destruction," Deep Throat said.

"But *why*?" Mulder's voice was agonized.

"The great powers did not want their power threatened by anything they could not control," said Deep Throat.

"But that's . . . that's . . ." Mulder tried to find the right word.

"That's life on earth," Deep Throat said. "And
I—"

His voice wavered and trailed off.

Mulder could only wait for him to summon up
the inner resources to go on.

Finally he did. "I . . . I have the distinction of being
one of three men who destroyed such a creature."

"You?" said Mulder. "Where? When?"

"I was with the CIA in Vietnam," said Deep
Throat. "A UFO had been seen in the sky for five
nights. The marines shot it down and brought it
to us."

"You actually saw it?" Mulder's voice quivered
with excitement.

"Maybe it didn't know what a gun was," Deep
Throat said. "Or maybe they don't show emotion.
But its innocent and blank expression has haunted
me—until I found you."

Deep Throat moved toward Mulder now.

Mulder felt an impulse to retreat. But he held
his ground—and felt the overwhelming sorrow that
flowed out of Deep Throat's eyes penetrating his
very soul.

"That's why I come to you, Mr. Mulder," Deep
Throat said, stopping barely three feet away. "That's
why I will continue to come to you. Through you, I
may make up for what I have done. Through you,
someday, perhaps the truth will be known."

With a mournful step, Deep Throat moved toward the glassed-in chamber. His heart pounding so hard it hurt, Mulder went with him.

Side by side the men looked through the glass.

The chamber was empty.

Mulder turned away, empty as well.

The whole laboratory seemed empty, of sound, of life, of hope.

Silently Deep Throat left the room.

Wordlessly Mulder followed—down the deserted corridor and down in the elevator to ground level.

They walked out of the building and stood in the cold rain that had begun to fall. Mulder barely felt it. He was numb from head to toe.

"You're awfully quiet, Mr. Mulder," Deep Throat said.

"I'm just wondering," Mulder said.

"Wondering what?" Deep Throat asked.

"Wondering which of your lies to believe," Mulder said coldly.

A ghost of what could have been a smile flickered briefly on Deep Throat's shadowed face.

"So I have been able to teach you something," he said. "Be patient. More will come."

Pulling his collar up around his neck, he walked off into the night.

"Mulder," said Scully's voice.

He turned. Two MPs were releasing her.

She joined Mulder in the slanting rain, but his attention was already focused elsewhere. She followed his gaze, and her eyes fell on Deep Throat's shadow.

Together they watched as the mysterious man disappeared into the watery darkness, taking with him Mulder's hope of finding a real E.B.E.—at least this time.

The End

Don't miss the next book in
the **X - FILES** series:

#10 DIE, BUG, DIE!

The man stared at the cockroach.

The cockroach stared back—and started to race for cover.

The man was too fast. His hand shot out and grabbed the cockroach scampering up the cement basement wall.

The man held the roach up, keeping it between his thumb and index finger. It fluttered its antennas helplessly in the air.

"Behold the mighty cockroach," the man said. He sounded like a teacher fondly explaining his favorite subject. He looked like a teacher, too, with a white shirt and a thin black tie, dark slacks, and shiny black shoes. On the back of his shirt, though, was a picture of a roach. Beneath the cartoon, bright red letters spelled DR. BUGGER—EXTERMINATOR. Dr. Bugger cured households of pests, and he loved his work.

"Cockroaches have lived on Earth far longer than we humans," Dr. Bugger informed the man who had hired him, Jeff Eckerle. Eckerle called himself a doctor, too, though the only thing he tried to heal was the environment. He was working to produce nonpolluting artificial fuel. He was a whiz in the lab. But right now, as he stared bug-eyed at the roach in Dr. Bugger's hand, what he was, was nervous.

"Scientists believe that roaches date from three hundred fifty million years ago," Dr. Bugger went on. "Today they can be found all over the world—from the tropics to the Arctic. There are over four thousand known varieties of them, and their numbers keep growing. In a year, a single female can produce over half a million offspring."

Dr. Bugger gazed affectionately at the roach wiggling desperately in his grip. Then he continued, "Nothing can get rid of them completely. They adapt to one poison after another. Even radiation does not kill them. In terms of survival, they are nearly perfect creatures. But of course, that is all they are—simple creatures. They can seek food. They can flee danger. But unlike humans, they cannot think."

"Thank goodness for that," said Dr. Eckerle. His light blue eyes were fixed on the roach. His pale face was even paler than usual.

"Yes," said Dr. Bugger. "Compared to roaches we are like gods. And we can act like gods as well."

With that, Dr. Bugger dropped the roach on the concrete floor. Before it could make a move, Dr. Bugger stomped it. At the crunching of its shell Dr. Eckerle winced, disgusted.

"Yuck," he said, gazing down at the remains. "You sure it's dead?"

"As a doornail," Dr. Bugger assured him.

"I've heard that even if you chop off their heads, they keep living," Dr. Eckerle said, still jittery. "It just takes them time to die of starvation."

Dr. Bugger shrugged. "Look, buddy, I don't know about that weird stuff. I just kill 'em."

"That's why I hired you," Dr. Eckerle said, still gazing squeamishly at the crushed roach.

"Then watch me go to work," Dr. Bugger said. "We'll be done in no time at all."

Dr. Bugger stooped over and picked up a spray tank. He started spraying the pesticide into cracks in the wall.

"I thought nowadays you froze the bugs to death," Dr. Eckerle said.

"Freeze them? Where's the fun in that?" Dr. Bugger asked. "Now we have a chemical that grows like a fungus. It not only gets rid of the roach that touches it but spreads to any other roach the first roach comes in contact with. This way, the bugs do all the work."

"Just as long as they disappear," Dr. Eckerle said. "If you don't mind, I think I'll skip the show. Bugs drive me crazy." With a shudder, he headed up the stairs.

The exterminator was grinning as he got down to work. Suddenly his smile vanished. He scowled at a roach on the wall in front of his face. The roach didn't make a move to run away. It actually seemed to be looking at Dr. Bugger defiantly, daring him to try to kill it.

"Why, you arrogant little—" Dr. Bugger snarled, and let loose a squirt of spray. It hit right on target.

The bug didn't lose its grip on the wall. In fact, it didn't seemed harmed at all. It did seem annoyed, though. At least the sharp chirp it made didn't sound very happy.

"I'm gonna have to find a new spray, I guess," Dr. Bugger muttered. "Until then . . ."

With the metal tip of his sprayer he knocked the roach off the wall, then brought his shoe down on top of it.

"When all else fails, nothing beats direct action," he said. Then he lifted his foot, and his mouth dropped open.

He watched as the bug scampered away unscathed.

"Oh, no you don't," Dr. Bugger said, and, moving

full speed, chased it down before it could reach cover.

This time he stomped it with all his force.

"Ow!" he cried. It felt as if a nail had gone through the sole of his shoe. He was half blind with pain. Grimacing, he tried to shake it off. He tried to go back to work. He squinted at chinks in the wall, looking for more roaches.

He saw them. Unflinchingly they stared back at him, just the way the last one had.

They saw him stagger backward, dropping his sprayer. They saw him clutch at his chest, then collapse against a wall.

Through a haze of agony Dr. Bugger saw their feelers waving gently in the air. It was as if they were waving good-bye.

That was the last thing Dr. Bugger saw. Ever.

His body lay still as the roaches came down out of the walls and crawled all over him.

It didn't disturb the roaches in the least when Dr. Eckerle came down the stairs saying, "Oh, I forgot to tell you I also found a roach in the—"

They did not even react when he started screaming.

TOP SECRET

CLASSIFIED

FOR INFORMATION ABOUT THE OFFICIAL X-FILES FAN CLUB CONTACT:

Creation Entertainment
411 N. Central Avenue
Suite 300
Glendale, CA 91203
(818) 409-0960

For more information about The X-Files or HarperCollins books visit our web site at: http://www.harpercollins.com/kids

THE Ⓧ FILES ™